It Figures!

FUN FIGURES OF SPEECH

It Figures!
FUN FIGURES OF SPEECH

by Marvin Terban
Illustrated by Giulio Maestro

CLARION BOOKS · NEW YORK

To my brothers-in-law,
George Freedman and Lewis Youngman,
who always cut fine figures.

Clarion Books
a Houghton Mifflin Company imprint
215 Park Avenue South, New York, NY 10003
Text copyright © 1993 by Marvin Terban
Illustrations copyright © 1993 by Giulio Maestro

Printed in the U.S.A.

Library of Congress Cataloging-in-Publication Data
Terban, Marvin.
It figures! : fun figures of speech / by Marvin Terban ; illustrated
by Giulio Maestro.
p.   cm.
Includes bibliographical references
Summary: Introduces and explains common figures of speech
such as metaphors, similes, personification, and hyperbole with
guidelines for their use and illustrative examples.
ISBN 0-395-61584-4   PA ISBN 0-395-66591-4
1. English language—Style—Juvenile literature.   2. Figures of
speech—Juvenile literature.   [1. English language—Style.
2. Figures of speech.]   I. Maestro, Giulio, ill.   II. Title.
PE1421.T45   1993
808'.042—dc20   92-35529
CIP   AC

EB 25 24 23 22 21 20 19 18

4500416665

Contents

FIGURING IT OUT

For as long as good writers have been putting their quill pens or lead pencils or word processors to paper, they have tried to express themselves in the most colorful, imaginative, descriptive ways possible.

They have tried to create lively, rich word pictures so that their readers could see the images and understand the feelings they were writing about. They have tried to give their readers the taste and smell and feel and sound and look of the scenes they were describing. They have tried to give vivid expression to their feelings and thoughts about people, places, things, and events so that their readers could share these impressions.

To write vividly, writers often use *figures of speech*. Figures of speech are special ways of putting words and phrases together to give strong, sharp, clear impressions. This book will introduce you to six of the most frequently used figures of speech and suggest ways that you can use them.

Don't confuse *figures of speech* with *the parts of speech*. The parts of speech are words. Figures of speech are imaginative expressions.

The Parts of Speech	**Figures of Speech**
noun (candle)	simile
verb (shouted)	metaphor
adjective (amazing)	hyperbole
adverb (wildly)	personification
pronoun (he)	onomatopoeia
preposition (in)	alliteration
interjection (gadzooks!)	(and many more)
conjunction (and)	

You always use the parts of speech to write sentences that sometimes contain figures of speech:

"Gadzooks!" he shouted wildly during the amazing eclipse. "The sun just went out like a candle in the wind!"

"The sun went out like a candle in the wind" is a perfect example of one of the most popular figures of speech, a *simile* (SIM-uh-lee). You'll learn more about similes and five other figures of speech in this book.

Even though these word combinations are called figures of *speech,* they're used most often in writing. That's because when you write, you have more time to think about how you want to express yourself—more time to revise, refine, and polish your ideas—than when you're just talking. You can use figures of speech to enrich your speech as well, but becoming a more original, dynamic writer is a good way to begin. Write on!

SIMILES
Are Like . . .

Let's say you're writing a story and you want to describe your bedroom the night the heat went off. You might write, "My room was cold." That's a perfectly good sentence. Or you might want to try to express yourself a little more creatively by writing, "My room was as cold as ice." This is a *simile* (SIM-uh-lee). It's a comparison between the coldness of your room and the coldness of ice. It helps your readers really get the feel of just how cold your room was. Notice that the word *as* is in the simile.

In your story, the lady next door is wearing a new hat with fake fruit on it. You could write, "Her hat had a lot of fake fruit on it," or you could express yourself more figuratively by writing

"Her hat looked like a fruit bowl," another simile. You are comparing your neighbor's hat with a bowl of fruit. That simile helps your readers get a good image of just what the hat looked like. Notice that the word *like* is in the simile.

Similes are lively comparisons used to enrich descriptions of people, places, things, emotions, and actions. A simile links two different elements by comparing one with the other in a way that shows how they are actually alike. Readers and listeners know what the two things are (a bedroom and ice; a hat and a fruit bowl), even though they don't usually think of them together. When you use a simile, you are pointing out some quality or characteristic (color, size, shape, movement, texture, smell, action, emotion, taste, etc.) that the two different things have in common.

A simile always contains either the word *like* or the word *as*, because the writer is saying that something is like or the same as something else.

Although you probably didn't realize it before, you already know some similes very well.

Mary had a little lamb,
Its **fleece was white as snow** . . .

Sarah Josepha Hale, "Mary's Lamb"

Here the poet used a simile to say that the lamb's wool was the same color as snow.

And **he looked like a peddler** just opening his pack.
His eyes, how they twinkled! his dimples, how merry!
His **cheeks were like roses,** his **nose like a cherry;**
His droll little **mouth was drawn up like a bow,**
And the **beard** on his chin **was as white as the snow.**

Clement Clarke Moore, "A Visit from St. Nicholas"

In this one stanza above, the writer used five similes (four with *like* and one with *as*) to tell you that Santa Claus's actions were like those of a peddler, that his cheeks and nose had the same red color as roses and a cherry, that his mouth had the same shape as a bow, and that, like the fleece on Mary's lamb, Santa's beard was the same color as snow.

Twinkle, twinkle, **little star,**
How I wonder what you are,
Up above the world so high,
Like a diamond in the sky!

Jane Taylor, "The Star"

This poet said that a star in the sky shines and sparkles like a diamond that catches the light.

. . . as snug as a bug in a rug.

Benjamin Franklin

The noted American statesman and inventor made up this famous simile. He was comparing being comfy and cozy to being a tiny insect, safe and secure in a soft, thick carpet or blanket. (In Ben Franklin's time, *rug* meant both.)

Neatly upon his left ear on the callous pavement two waiters pitched Soapy. **He arose joint by joint, as a carpenter's rule opens . . .**

O. Henry, "The Cop and the Anthem"

In the last sentence above, the great American short story writer O. Henry compared the actions of a man getting up from the sidewalk, limb by limb, to a carpenter's hinged ruler opening section by section.

Because people have been using effective similes for centuries, there are many similes that have become well known. Here are examples of some of these popular and expressive comparisons. You'll notice that people are sometimes compared to animals. That's because writers often think that people act or look the way animals act or look. And people really are animals, after all.

In the morning, **he moves like a snail.** No wonder he's always late.

As quick as a wink, he grabbed the cookie and was out the door.

Don't **stand there like a statue.** Do something.

To support her family, **she works like a horse.**

Even in the face of danger, **she's as cool as a cucumber.**

12

About Clichés

An often-used and familiar expression is called a *cliché* (klee-SHAY). Creative people usually try to avoid clichés because these expressions are not new. They try to think up their own original images instead. In your writing, you may not always want to repeat a simile that someone else made up a long time ago and that most people know today.

You can turn an overused saying into something newer and fresher by adding to or changing the word picture. Try to express the comparison in an inventive way that you think your readers will understand and enjoy. Just make sure your new simile works and fits in with what you're writing.

For instance, "cold as ice" is a cliché. You might describe the coldness of your room a little more imaginatively by saying, "My room was as cold as a North Pole iceberg," or "My room was as cold as a witch's heart," or "My room was as cold as an air-conditioned igloo," or "My room was as cold as a snowman's toes." Instead of writing "as cool as a cucumber," which is another cliché, try to think of something else that's cool. How about, "as cool as an autumn breeze," or "as cool as a forgotten cup of tea"?

Here are some familiar clichés changed into new similes.

Shhh! Try to **be as quiet as a mouse.**
     . . . as quiet as a crater on the moon.

Come on! Move your feet. **You're as slow as molasses.**
**. . . as slow as new
ketchup.**

On this new mattress, **you'll sleep like a baby.**
**. . . sleep like a moving man
on vacation.**

This **professor is as dull as dishwater.**
. . . as dull as dust.

Be creative. Surprise your readers by making them see every-day things in new and unusual ways. Maybe some of the similes you make up today will be so terrific that years from now, other people will be using them and they will be clichés!

Here are three new similes that compare a place, an action, and people to other things.

Pick up your dirty laundry. Your **room smells like a skunks' hotel.**

Going into the principal's office when she's angry **is as dangerous as walking a tightrope over a volcano.**

The restless **children were hopping about like kernels in a corn popper.**

Now, try your hand at making up some similes of your own. Here are a few ideas to get you started. Try your best to avoid clichés. If you've heard or read an expression before, think about how you could change it to make it your own. Some suggestions are on page 16.

1. He can flip a pizza as fast as . . .
2. This new feather pillow is as fluffy as . . .
3. It was so hectic at the mall, people were running around like . . .
4. Sometimes I think my brother's brain is as tiny as . . .
5. The children rushed to Grandma's newly baked cookies like . . .

Clowning Around with Figures of Speech

Suppose your teacher gives the class an assignment to write a paper describing a favorite character. You choose a clown you saw at the circus. You start by writing:

The clown was nice. She looked and acted funny. She made everyone at the circus laugh.

That's an OK beginning, but wouldn't your paper be livelier if you added some figures of speech? You could start with a few similes.

The clown's smile could make your **face light up like fireworks on the Fourth of July.** Her **hair was like green spaghetti,** her **nose was like a red lightbulb,** her **feet were like large pancakes with toes,** and her **stomach was like a laundry sack full of doorknobs.** She acted funny and made everyone at the circus laugh.

These are the author's ideas for finishing the similes on page 15, but yours are just as good.

1. a kid can spend a dollar.
2. a cloud rinsed in fabric softener.
3. mechanical toys with overcharged batteries.
4. the period at the end of this sentence.
5. bits of iron to a magnet.

METAPHORS
Are . . .

Metaphors (MET-uh-forz) are like similes, but with one big difference.

Like a simile, a metaphor describes a person, place, thing, feeling, idea, or action by comparing it to something else. But a metaphor does not have the word *like* or the word *as* in it.

For instance, Rachel is very smart. She's positively brilliant. If you wanted to describe Rachel with a simile, you could say, "Rachel is like a talking encyclopedia." To use a metaphor, you could say, "Rachel is a talking encyclopedia." You're still comparing Rachel to an encyclopedia. The word picture is just as vivid. But you've left out the word *like*.

A simile says that one thing is *like* another thing. A metaphor says one thing *is* another thing (figuratively speaking, of course). A metaphor is more direct than a simile.

Simile: Eddie eats like a hog.
Metaphor: Eddie is a hog.

Remember the cold room from the last chapter? Well, instead of writing, "My room was as cold as ice" (simile), you could write, "My room was an icebox" (metaphor). You don't even have to use *is* or *was.* You could write, "My sister sleeps in a toaster oven and I sleep in an icebox!" Your readers will get the metaphorical picture.

Avoiding Mixed Metaphors
or, How Not to Swim a Mountain

Let's say you're writing a letter to your pen pal. You want to tell him or her how tough your school is and how much work your teachers give you. You're feeling creative, so you write:

Every day, I have to swim a mountain of schoolwork. Every night, I have to climb a sea of homework.

Something's wrong with those two metaphors. Can you figure out what it is? (Hint: Try to make real pictures in your mind out of the exact words and you'll probably spot the errors quickly. Can you swim a mountain? Can you climb a sea?)

Metaphors like those above, that combine things that don't make sense together, are called *mixed metaphors*. Mixing up parts of a metaphor is a common mistake. Even experienced writers and speakers do it sometimes. But they (and you) should try to avoid it.

Here are corrected versions of the mixed-up homework metaphors:

Every day, I have to swim a sea of schoolwork. (*Swim* and *sea* make sense together.)

Every night, I have to climb a mountain of homework. (*Climb* and *mountain* make sense together.)

When you decide to use a metaphor in your writing, analyze it carefully. Ask yourself if all parts of the figurative word picture you are trying to paint really make sense together and belong in the same picture. If not, you've probably written a mixed metaphor. That can confuse your readers. Try to rethink your metaphor and unmix it.

Here are more examples of mixed metaphors. Think about how you could correct them. Then turn to page 24 for the un-mixed-up versions.

1. She worked hard and rode up the ladder of success. (Hint: How do you get up a ladder?)

2. The governor is a captain who steers the ship of state, sometimes through turbulent air pockets. (Hint: When you steer a ship on water, do you hit air pockets?)
3. This algebra problem is really complicated, and every time I think I'm out of the maze, I sink to the bottom. (Hint: Can you sink in a maze?)

Many writers and poets have used metaphors. William Shakespeare, probably the best-known writer in the world, used them all the time.

> I will not change my horse with any that treads . . .
> When I bestride him, I soar, **I am a hawk.**
>
> *King Henry V*

Here Shakespeare wrote that when the rider is on top of the horse, he feels that he is a bird, a hawk, high up and moving fast.

> All **the world's a stage,**
> And all **the men and women** merely **players.**
>
> *As You Like It*

In these famous lines Shakespeare compared the world to a stage in a theater and wrote that every person in the world is an actor performing on that stage.

But, soft! what light through yonder window breaks?
It is the East and **Juliet is the sun!**

Romeo and Juliet

Romeo, Juliet's boyfriend, was saying that his beloved Juliet, coming to her window, was as beautiful to him as the sun rising in the east.

Here are other examples of metaphors from great authors.

The wind was a torrent of darkness among the gusty trees,
The moon was a ghostly galleon tossed upon cloudy seas,
The road was a ribbon of moonlight over the purple moor,
And the highwayman came riding—
    Riding—riding—
The highwayman came riding, up to the old inn-door.

Alfred Noyes, "The Highwayman"

A good laugh is sunshine in a house.

William Makepeace Thackeray

Just like similes, well-known metaphors can become clichés, too. For instance, many writers have used metaphors to compare life to a road ("As they traveled down the path of life together . . ."), or to a day ("In the twilight of his life, when he was old . . ."), or to a year ("In the springtime of her youth . . ."), or to flowing water ("As I sailed the sea of life . . ."). Those are good metaphors that got a little overused.

Here are some other popular metaphors that people have enjoyed for a long time. Remember, however, that because they've been used so often before, they're clichés. Try your best to think up your own metaphors when you write so your writing will be original and fresh.

A **blanket of snow** covered the village.

On the day of the fair, the **schoolyard was a beehive of activity.**

We're all **in the same boat,** so let's row together.

The way he eats, you'd think his **stomach was a bottomless pit.**

Here are some sentences with metaphors that are not clichés (yet).

"My dog's **fur is a shag rug.**"
   "You think that's bad? My dog's **fur is an overgrown lawn.** I don't know whether to get out the scissors or the lawn mower!"

During the storm, the roaring **wind choreographed a ballet** of old newspapers on the street.

When it comes to describing something, which figurative comparison should you use—a simile or a metaphor? Both figures of speech can help your readers see common objects, feelings, and actions in creative and fresh ways. Try both kinds in the story or poem you're trying to write and see which one you like better. You could use a simile in one part and a metaphor in the next.

It's time to try creating a few new metaphors of your own. Below are some situations you might want to write about. Think about how you could describe them figuratively using metaphors. Compare each of the objects, scenes, and actions below to something else that's unexpected but still similar in some way. Some metaphorical suggestions are given on page 24.

1. Clouds
2. A book whose stories introduce the reader to new subjects
3. A bell in a tower that wakes you up every morning
4. An angry revolution that starts small and becomes big
5. A snowstorm

Clowning Around (continued)

Remember the story you were writing about the clown? Now you could add a metaphor to it.

The clown was a one-woman laughter machine. Her smile could make your face light up like fireworks on the Fourth of July. Her hair was like green spaghetti, her nose was like a red lightbulb, her feet were like large pancakes with toes, and her stomach was like a laundry sack full of doorknobs. She acted funny and made everyone at the circus laugh.

Unmixed-up metaphors from page 19:

1. She worked hard and climbed up the ladder of success.
2. The governor is a captain who steers the ship of state, sometimes through rough waters.
3. This algebra problem is really complicated, and every time I think I'm out of the maze, I bump into a wall.

Suggestions for new metaphors from page 23, but your ideas are just as good.

1. The lost plane flew into **clouds of gray wool** and vanished.
2. The **book was a spaceship** that transported him to strange worlds.
3. The **town hall bell is my morning alarm clock.**
4. The **flames of revolution** started out as **small brushfires** but turned into **raging infernos** that spread throughout the country.
5. When the snowstorm started, the little girl imagined that some giant had tipped a **big bowl of white cornflakes** upside down on her.

ONOMATOPOEIA
Sound Effects in Your Writing

Shh! Just for a moment, freeze. Close your eyes if you can. Concentrate only on the sounds you hear—a pencil sharpener, kitchen appliances, a fan, people.

Go outside. Listen to all the sounds of traffic and nature—trucks, crowds, animals, the wind.

Now here comes the challenge for you, the writer: to think of words that capture the sounds of sounds.

Drop a stone into water. Hear that sound? Is it plop? Splish? Splash? Step into snow. What word imitates that exact sound your boots make? Is it crunch? Squish? Chew your cereal. What words recreate those sounds in your mouth? Are they snap, crackle, and pop? Or bang, gurgle, and whizz? Touch things together. Do you hear clink, clank, clunk, or some other sound?

25

Almost since talking and writing began, speakers and authors have been creating words that sound like sounds. They want their listeners and readers to experience not only the look, smell, taste, and feel of things, but also their sounds.

Making up these "soundwords" isn't easy. There are millions of sounds in the world, but in the English language there are only forty-four sounds and only twenty-six letters to write those sounds down with. It's a real challenge to put letters together in just the right way to form a word that imitates a sound.

The figure of speech that means to form words that sound like sounds is called *onomatopoeia* (on-uh-mat-uh-PEE-uh). That six-syllable mouthful of a word comes from Greek and means "to make up names"—the names of sounds. You may not realize it, but you read and hear and use onomatopoetic words every day.

Someone once heard a bird sing and tried to make up a word that imitated the bird's song. To that person it sounded like *whippoorwill*, and that onomatopoetic word became the bird's name. (Its official Latin name is *Caprimulgus vociferus*, but isn't "whippoorwill" much more beautiful?)

Someone was listening to the sound a broom made as it moved across the floor. This writer wrote down a word to imitate that sound—*sweep*. That word is so common today, it's easy to forget that it is an onomatopoetic word, a word that copies a sound.

A writer who wanted to capture the sound of a sneeze in a word wrote *achoo!* That word does sound like a sneeze, doesn't it?

Even very young children use onomatopoeia. When you were little, your parents or grandparents probably asked you, "What does a dog say?" and you probably answered, "Bow wow."

"What does a cat say?"
"Meow."

Bow wow and *meow* are onomatopoetic words because they imitate real sounds, the sounds animals make.

Onomatopoetic words that express animal sounds and other sounds in other languages are different from the English words. For example, in French, people say that dogs say "ouah-ouah." Spanish children say that dogs bark "guau-guau," and in Japanese it's "wung-wung."

Here are some examples from the works of famous writers of onomatopoeia:

Baa, baa, black sheep,
Have you any wool?
Yes, sir, yes, sir,
Three bags full . . .
                    "Mother Goose"

Hear the sledges with the bells—
Silver bells!
What a world of merriment their melody foretells!
How they **tinkle, tinkle, tinkle,**
In the icy air of night!
While the stars that oversprinkle
All the heavens, seems to twinkle
With a crystalline delight;
Keeping time, time, time,
In a sort of Runic rhyme,
To the **tintinnabulation** that so musically wells
From the bells, bells, bells, bells,
Bells, bells, bells—
From the **jingling** and the **tinkling** of the bells.
                    Edgar Allan Poe, "The Bells"

The ice was here, the ice was there,
The ice was all around:
It **cracked** and **growled**, and **roared** and **howled**,
Like noises in a swound!

> Samuel Taylor Coleridge, "Rime of the Ancient Mariner"

Swound is an old-fashioned spelling of *swoon*, which means "faint."

People who write comic books use onomatopoeia all the time.

You might be wondering when you should use onomatopoeia. In descriptive writing, you may want to give your readers a complete sense impression of a scene—including sound effects. That's when you use onomatopoeia.

Now you can spot onomatopoeia in everyday writing:

The **blip** on the radar screen alerted the agents to the approach of the spy plane.

From the sharp **crack** of the bat as it **whacked** the ball, she knew it was a home run.

"Come here, pretty fly," **murmured** the spider.

When his stomach **rumbles,** he knows it's time to eat.

Give onomatopoeia a try. What words can you think of that will recreate, capture, or imitate the following sounds? You'll find some possible answers on page 32.

1. A soda can being opened
2. Coins being tossed into a glass
3. A foot stepping into a wet sneaker
4. Someone snoring
5. Car brakes pressed rapidly

When you write, you can use words you've heard or read before, or you can make up your own onomatopoetic words as people have done for centuries. Just put letters together to form brand new words that copy the sounds you hear—words like **kerplosh, sizzkrunk,** and **bamblam.** If you make up the right word, then someone who reads your poem, story, essay, or article will hear the same sound you heard when you wrote that word down. Doesn't that sound good?

Clowning Around (continued again)

Now you can put a few examples of onomatopoeia into your description of the clown to help your readers hear the sounds of the circus.

The clown was a one-woman laughter machine. Her smile could make your face light up like fireworks on the Fourth of July. Her hair was like green spaghetti, her nose was like a red lightbulb, her feet were like large pancakes with toes, and her stomach was like a laundry sack full of door-knobs. Children **howled** with glee when she made the horn go **toot,** the cannon go **boom,** and the cream pie go **splat!** When you squeezed her nose, it **blurped!** She made every-one at the circus laugh.

Some possible answers to the onomatopoeia challenge on page 30, but remember that the words you made up could be just as good.

1. pop; fizzz
2. ping-plink
3. squish
4. awrk-fnoof-zzzz
5. screeeech

ALLITERATION
Wonderful Words That Certainly Sound Super

Betty Botter bought some butter.
"But," she said, "the butter's bitter.
If I bake it in my batter,
Bitter will my batter be."

What's the first thing that you notice about that tongue twister? Twelve of the twenty-three words begin with a b sound. Now you know what *alliteration* (uh-lit-uh-RAY-shun) is. Putting together two or more words that begin with the same sound is called alliteration.

It's just the first *sound* that has to be the same, not necessarily the *letter*. For instance, c and k sometimes make the same sound, so "candy kitchen" and "ketchup container" are examples of alliteration. So are "funny phone," "generous judge,"

"six cents," and "psychology student." The first sounds in these phrases are the same, even though the first letters are not.

On the other hand, the following phrases are not, strictly speaking, alliteration: "honest Henry," "church choir," "cracked ceiling," and "whole whale." The initial letters are the same, but not the initial sounds.

Some of your favorite cartoon, movie, and storybook characters have alliterative names: Donald and Daisy Duck, Mickey and Minnie Mouse, Bugs Bunny, Betty Boop, Roger Rabbit, Huckleberry Hound, King Kong, Jack and Jill, Simple Simon, (Old) King Cole, Wee Willie Winkie, (Little) Miss Muffet, and (Little) Boy Blue. Alliteration makes these names fun to say and easier to remember.

Four presidents of the United States in the twentieth century had names that were alliterative. Their parents must have liked the way their children's names sounded. Can you name them?

☆ CLUES TO ☆ ALLITERATIVE U.S. PRESIDENTS:

Initials: **W. W.**
Our twenty-eighth president, 1913-1921, held the office during World War I.

Initials: **C. C.**
Our thirtieth president, 1923-1929, served in more elective offices than any other.

Initials: **H. H.**
Our thirty-first president, 1929-1933, held office at the beginning of the Great Depression.

Initials: **R. R.**
Our fortieth president, 1981–1988, had been an actor in Hollywood and a state governor.

The answers are upside down at the bottom of this page.

Woodrow Wilson   Calvin Coolidge   Herbert Hoover   Ronald Reagan

Many well-known tongue twisters contain alliteration:

Peter **P**iper **p**icked a **p**eck of **p**ickled **p**eppers . . .

She **s**ells **s**ea**sh**ells by the **s**ea**sh**ore . . .

A **t**utor who **t**ooted a flute
Tried **t**o **t**each **t**wo young **t**ooters **t**o **t**oot . . .

Some beloved nursery rhymes are also alliterative:

Peter, **P**eter, **P**umpkin-eater . . .

Georgie **P**orgie, **p**udding and **p**ie . . .

Sing a **s**ong of **s**ixpence . . .

Mary, **M**ary, **q**uite **c**ontrary,
How does your **g**arden **g**row? . . .

A popular jump-rope chant, "A my name is Alice," contains a lot of alliteration. Kids have fun making up the words as they jump. An example: "**J** my name is **J**ennifer. My husband's name is **J**ack. I come from **J**amaica and I sell **j**ellybeans."

In "The Star-Spangled Banner," our national anthem, Francis Scott Key achieved a neat bit of double alliteration when he wrote about "**br**oad **st**ripes and **br**ight **st**ars."

Many other writers have used alliteration to add fun, drama, or vivid sounds to their writing. Here are some examples.

"The time has come," the Walrus said,
"To talk of many things:
Of **sh**oes—and **sh**ips—and sealing wax
Of **c**abbages—and **k**ings— . . ."
                  Lewis Carroll, "The Walrus and the Carpenter"

Meanwhile, his friend, through alley and street,
Wanders and **w**atches with **ea**ger **ea**rs,
Till in the silence around **h**im **h**e **h**ears
The **m**uster of **m**en at the barrack door, . . .
And **l**o! as he **l**ooks, on the belfry's height
A **gl**immer, and then a **gl**eam of light!
                 Henry Wadsworth Longfellow, "Paul Revere's Ride"

Love's **L**abour's **L**ost
    The title of a play by William Shakespeare

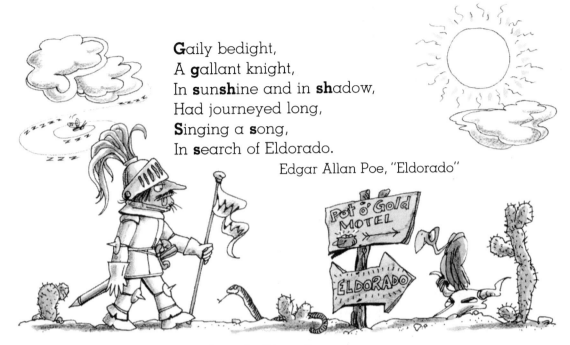

Gaily bedight,
A **g**allant knight,
In **s**un**sh**ine and in **sh**adow,
Had journeyed long,
Singing a **s**ong,
In **s**earch of Eldorado.

Edgar Allan Poe, "Eldorado"

Here are more examples of alliteration:

"**H**elp!" **h**ollered **H**arry as **h**e **h**ung **h**elplessly from the **h**elicopter in the **h**urricane.

George **J**ackson, the **j**olly **j**uggler, is a **g**enuine **g**enius.

My, isn't **M**artha's **m**acaroni **m**outhwatering, **m**adame?

37

Now **kn**eel, **n**oble **kn**ight, on your **kn**obby **kn**ees.

Vampires are **v**icious **v**illains.

You may be wondering how you can find lots of words that begin with the same sound and make sense together.

Start by thinking of a word you'd like to use. Then, from your own vocabulary, try to think of words with the same initial sound as that word. Perhaps you could say the word aloud and keep repeating the first sound until other words that begin with that same sound come to mind. Try different possibilities until you have two or three words that sound right together and make sense in the context of what you're writing.

If you run out of ideas, open any dictionary to words that begin with the sound you're trying to match. Let your eyes scan the pages. You should be able to pick out some suitable words that way.

Write down all the words as you think of them or find them in the dictionary. Keep trying different combinations of words until you compose your perfect alliterative phrase. But be sure that it makes sense in the context of your story, poem, song, cheer, or whatever you're writing.

When should you use alliteration in your writing? Use it when you want to add drama ("wild winter wind") or humor ("Petunia put purple pickles in the parakeet's pasta!"), or capture a sound ("sizzling sausages"), or give a character a memorable name ("Willy Wiggles"), or set a vivid scene ("The raging river roared over the ragged rocks"), or label something ("David's Dirty Duds"). Not every word has to begin with the same sound. But if at least two close together do, that's alliteration.

And, of course, don't overdo it. Alliteration is fun to use, but a little bit goes a long way. Too much could become totally and terribly tiresome to your reader. And misplaced alliteration (putting a funny name into a serious story, for instance) could spoil your writing. Use just a bit of alliteration here and there for good effect.

Clowning Around (more continuation)

Back to the clown story. You can now add a bit of alliteration to give your character a memorable name and for extra fun.

Clara the **C**razy **C**lown was a one-woman laughter machine. Her smile could make your face light up like fireworks on the Fourth of July. Her hair was like green spaghetti, her nose was like a red lightbulb, her feet were like large pancakes with toes, and her **b**elly **b**ulged like a laundry **b**ag **b**ursting with **b**owling **b**alls. Children **h**owled and **h**ollered when Clara made the horn go toot, the cannon go boom, and the cream pie go splat! When you squeezed her nose, it blurped! She made everyone at the circus laugh.

HYPERBOLE
Is the Best Thing Ever Invented in the Entire History of the World

Let's say you were up late doing your homework. The next day in school, you said to your friend, "I'm really tired." But if you wanted to use a fun figure of speech and express yourself more graphically, you could have said, "I'm so tired, I could sleep forever." Of course, you couldn't really sleep forever. Even Rip Van Winkle slept for only twenty years. But you could certainly describe how tired you were with an expressive phrase.

That figure of speech is called *hyperbole*. (This is a four-syllable word pronounced hye-PER-buh-lee.) "Hyperbole" comes from Greek and means "excess" or anything that goes beyond normal, believable limits. When you use a very big, extravagant, unbelievable exaggeration to express yourself, you're using hyperbole.

Writers use hyperbole when they want to express an idea or describe a scene in a way that's surprising ("It's so hot out there today, folks, the sidewalks are bubbling"); dramatic ("When they heard the fire alarm, the children rushed frantically out the door, like a herd of stampeding buffalo"); or humorous ("My cousin has such a big nose, you could hang a swing from it").

Readers don't take examples of hyperbole seriously, of course. They know the writer is obviously exaggerating outrageously to get a point across in a striking manner.

Classic examples of hyperbole appear over and over again in tall tales, a popular kind of American storytelling. Probably the most famous tall tales are told about the giant, superhuman Hercules of a lumberjack, Paul Bunyan. No task was too difficult for this clever mythical hero to perform in the great forests of frontier America. Marvelous stories have been told about how Paul singlehandedly dug the Columbia River to provide a log chute to the ocean; of how he built a bunkhouse so tall that the top seven floors had to be hinged to let the moon pass by each night; and how his footprints and those of his great blue ox, Babe, filled with water and became the ten thousand lakes of Minnesota. Readers know better than to take these wild folktales at face value. The fun in reading them comes from their hyperbolic excess. You could write tall tales like these and load them with hyperbole to delight your readers.

Here are some everyday examples of hyperbole:

My bookbag **weighs a ton.**

She opened the window and **ten billion mosquitoes** flew in.

If I've told you once, **I've told you a thousand times,** don't do that!

Dear David,
The water at my summer camp is so freezing in the morning that **little ice cubes come out of the showerheads.** And the mattresses feel like they're **stuffed with rocks.**

The food. Ugh! It's definitely **left over from the dinosaur age.** Even the dinosaurs wouldn't eat it.

My counselor is really mean. We call her **Attila the Hun.**

The lake is **a mud puddle,** the bunks are made of **tissue paper,** it costs about **a million dollars** to go here, and the director just **escaped from the zoo** (the gorilla's cage). I love this camp.

Your friend,

Jennifer

Hyperbole has been used by many authors, songwriters, and poets. For example, you may know the famous song about the old lady who swallowed a fly. Then she swallowed a spider to catch the fly. Then she swallowed a bird, a cat, a dog, a cow, and finally a horse. She died, of course. Nobody believes any of that really happened, but those hyperboles are lots of fun to sing. Here are some other examples:

BOING

SPRONG

SPRING

ZOOM

I asked my mother for fifty cents
To see the elephant jump the fence.
He jumped so high that **he touched the sky,**
And never came back till the Fourth of July.

Old Joe Brown, he had a wife,
She was all of **eight feet tall.**
She slept with her **head in the kitchen,**
And her **feet stuck out in the hall.**

Anonymous American folk poems

45

I had a little husband,
No bigger than my thumb;
I put him in a pint pot
And then I bade him drum;
I gave him some garters
To garter up his hose,
And a little silk handkerchief
To wipe his pretty nose.

English nursery rhyme

Now it's time for you to try your hand at using hyperbole.
Below are some unfinished sentences. See what kind of exaggerated expressions you can come up with. Some of the author's ideas can be found on page 48.

1. I'm so thirsty I could . . .
2. It's so cold today that . . .
3. That woman is so tall that . . .
4. Wow, is your pet canary fat! Or is that a . . .?
5. This window fan is so incredibly powerful that we named it . . .

As with other figures of speech, a little hyperbole goes a long way (and that's not an exaggeration). But when you want to make an occasional far-out statement on purpose for humor or dramatic effect, try a bit of hyperbole.

Clowning Around (almost done)

A little hyperbole will add special effects to your description of Clara the Clown.

Clara the Crazy Clown was a one-woman laughter machine. Her smile was so big, **it went around her head a couple of times.** It could make your face light up like fireworks on the Fourth of July. Her hair was like green spaghetti, her nose was like a red lightbulb, her feet were like large pancakes with toes, and her belly bulged like a laundry bag bursting with bowling balls. Children howled and hollered when Clara made the horn go toot, the cannon go boom, and the cream pie go splat! When you squeezed her nose, it blurped! **The line of people waiting to get into the circus stretched a zillion miles** because Clara made everyone laugh.

These are the author's suggestions for adding hyperbole to the sentences on page 46, but your ideas are just as good.

1. drink the Atlantic and Pacific oceans dry!
2. even the snowman in the schoolyard is wearing long underwear.
3. she makes the Empire State Building look like a toy model.
4. yellow hippo with feathers?
5. "The Tornado" (or "The Hurricane" or "The Cyclone" or "The Typhoon").

PERSONIFICATION
Is Your Friend

When you look at a tree, what do you see? Roots, a trunk, limbs, branches, and leaves. Of course. But if you use your imagination, can you see that a tree is like a person standing up? The roots are like the feet on the ground. The trunk is like the body of the person. The limbs are like arms, the branches are like fingers, and the leaves could be the person's hair.

Poet Joyce Kilmer described a tree as if it were a person when he wrote in his poem, "Trees":

> A tree that looks at God all day,
> and lifts its leafy arms to pray; . . .

When a writer gives a thing (a tree) the qualities of a person (the ability to look up, raise one's arms, and pray), that's a figure of speech called *personification* (per-sohn-ih-fih-KAY-shun).

What are some of the qualities of a person? A person has a head with eyes, a nose, a mouth, ears, and hair. A person has a body with arms and legs, fingers and toes. A person can see, hear, touch, smell, and taste. A person can talk, walk, think, laugh, speak, and have all kinds of emotions.

Clouds, mountains, rivers, the wind, and the rain don't have any of these qualities. Neither do stars, earth, grass, flowers, a house, a car, a chair, a bed, a lamp, or a fan. But in the imagination of a writer—in your imagination—a thing, animal, or idea can have the qualities, characteristics, and personality of a person.

When you use personification, your words create very definite pictures by suggesting that things look or act like people. Personification helps the reader, who is a person, to identify with a thing that resembles or is behaving like a person.

Writers have often used personification to picture the elements of nature—the sun, the stars, the wind—as having the qualities of people. Mother Earth, Mother Nature, Father Time, Old Man Winter, The Man in the Moon, and Jack Frost are all well-known examples of personification.

Father Time   Mother Time

Baby Time

Late lies the wintry sun a-bed,
A frosty, fiery sleepy-head;
Blinks but an hour or two; and then,
A blood-red orange, sets again.

Robert Louis Stevenson, "Winter-Time"

Here the poet described the winter sun as a sleepy person who stays in bed late (and therefore rises late), blinks but an hour or two (stays up in the sky for a short time), and goes back to bed (sets early).

When the stars threw down their spears
And watered heaven with their tears,
Did he smile his work to see?
Did he who made the Lamb make thee?

William Blake, "The Tiger"

When the Dawn spread her fingertips of rose in the eastern sky, the men and dogs went hunting.

Homer, *The Odyssey*

Round the cape of a sudden came the sea,
And the sun looked over the mountain's rim . . .

Robert Browning, "Parting at Morning"

I saw you toss the kites on high
And blow the birds about the sky;
And all around I heard you pass,
Like ladies' skirts across the grass—
O wind, a-blowing all day long,
O wind, that sings so loud a song!

Robert Louis Stevenson, "The Wind"

Here are some examples of personification as it might be used in everyday writing:

The old college buildings looked as though they had grown thick beards of ivy since the last time I had visited the campus.

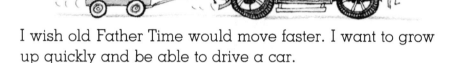

I wish old Father Time would move faster. I want to grow up quickly and be able to drive a car.

The picnic was a disaster. Nature doesn't like me. First the sun decided to take the day off. And when the wind smelled the hot dogs cooking, it rushed down to put out the flames of the barbecue. And the clouds opened up and pelted us with huge raindrops. We'll try again tomorrow.

A little personification can make your writing more interesting by helping the reader see an everyday thing in a more interesting way—as if that thing were a person. Your reader might never have thought of that thing in that way before.

Let's try it out. Here are some unfinished sentences. How could you finish them using personification? Some ideas are on page 56.

1. In the desert the huge cactus plants reminded him of . . . (What?)
2. "Never enter Dead Man's Canyon," she whispered. "It's the . . ." (What is it?)
3. The fearsome cyclone . . . (What did it do?)
4. He loved getting home after a long day at work and letting his favorite overstuffed chair . . . (Do what?)
5. I was on a diet, and all the pastries in the bakery window were . . . (Doing what?)

Try to personify a few objects in your writing. It will make what you write more personable. But don't get carried away with it. As with the other figures of speech in this book, personification is best when used sparingly.

Clowning Around (the last word)

Adding some personification to your paper on Clara the Crazy Clown will add the final figurative touch to your description of her.

Clara the Crazy Clown was a one-woman laughter machine. Her smile was so big, it went around her head a couple of times. It could make your face light up like fireworks on the Fourth of July. Her hair was like green spaghetti, her nose was like a red lightbulb, her feet were like large pancakes with toes, and her belly bulged like a laundry bag bursting with bowling balls. Children howled and hollered when Clara made the horn go toot, the cannon go boom, and the cream pie go splat! When you squeezed her nose, it blurped! The line of people waiting to get into the circus stretched a zillion miles because Clara made everyone laugh. Even in bad weather, when **Mother Nature hurled fiery thunderbolts** down at the Big Top or when **Jack Frost touched people with his icy fingers,** the audience flocked to see Clara and be warmed by her silly antics.

Here are some suggestions for personifications to finish the sentences on page 54, but any ideas you have are just as good as these.

1. people being held up by robbers.
2. mouth of the devil, and it swallows all who dare to venture in."
3. picked the tree up in its huge hands and hurled it into the next county.
4. hug him with its soft arms.
5. shouting, "Eat me! Eat me!"

It Figures!

Now you know what the six most commonly used figures of speech are. But how do you know when to use them to enliven and color your writing, and which ones to use?

Since you're the writer, that's really up to you. Use them when they fall naturally into your writing. Don't strain to use a figure of speech just because you think you should.

If you feel that a comparison will help your readers get the image you're trying to convey better, then try to think of a *simile* or *metaphor* to express yourself with a word picture like, "The cat's eyes, burning like cinders, watched me as I searched the cellar," or "She was a flower of a girl: her body was a slender stem, and her hair blossomed with curly red petals."

Perhaps you want to convey the sounds you'd like your readers to hear as they read your story. Write in some *onomatopoeia*: "He tried to creep silently up to the window, but the crackling and crunching of twigs under his feet revealed his presence."

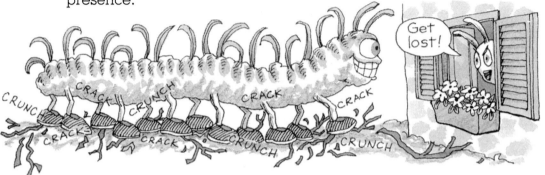

Want to give a character a memorable name ("King Carlos of Kartonia") or put some words together that are just fun to read aloud ("Sybil's Sensational Sodas")? Try a little *alliteration*.

If you want a character in one of your stories to make a dramatically exaggerated point, let her say something *hyperbolic* like, "A million charging hippos couldn't budge me from this spot!" Or if you want to describe some thing, person, or action with an exaggerated effect, you might write: "With muscles of forged iron and the strength of a giant crane, he lifted the fallen tree off the frightened puppy."

Sometimes you want to let your readers see how something in your story or poem seems like a person to you. *Personify* it and your readers will get the picture by identifying with the human qualities of that thing: "All the frightened flowers ran from the meadow when the tornado approached."

Just remember, don't overdo it. Try to avoid clichés and be as original as you can.

Sometimes two or more figures of speech can be worked into one piece of writing. In the sentence "The ferocious fire ate the forest like a ravenous fox devouring its prey," can you see examples of *alliteration* ("ferocious fire . . . forest . . . fox"), *personification* ("the . . . fire ate"), and *simile* ("like a hungry fox")?

When the poet Henry Wadsworth Longfellow wanted to describe a shower in his poem "Rain in Summer," he wrote:

> How it clatters along the roofs,
> Like the tramp of hoofs!
> How it gushes and struggles out
> From the throat of the overflowing spout!

Did you spot at least three figures of speech in those four lines? There is *onomatopoeia* ("clatters," "gushes," and "tramp"), *simile* ("clatters . . . like the tramp of hoofs"), and *personification* ("throat").

This book has introduced you to six of the most commonly used figures of speech. Starting now, try using *similes, metaphors, personification, hyperbole, alliteration,* and *onomatopoeia*. Your writing will be a lot more descriptive, interesting, lively, and colorful. It figures!

Bibliography

If you want to read more about figures of speech, you might like to look through some of the books the author used when writing this book.

Alexander, Arthur. *The Poet's Eye: An Introduction to Poetry for Young People.* Englewood Cliffs, NJ: Prentice Hall, Inc., 1967.

Hall, Susan. *Using Picture Storybooks to Teach Literary Devices.* Phoenix, AZ: Oryx Press, 1990.

Koch, Kenneth. *Wishes, Lies, and Dreams: Teaching Children to Write Poetry.* New York: Harper & Row, 1980.

Livingston, Myra Cohn. *Poem-Making: Ways to Begin Writing Poetry.* New York: HarperCollins Publishers, 1991.

———— . *When You Are Alone/It Keeps You Capone.* New York: Atheneum, 1973.

Wood, James Playsted. *Poetry Is.* Boston: Houghton Mifflin Company, 1972.

For a lighthearted look at other sides of our language,
see these Clarion Word Play Books
by **Marvin Terban**
with illustrations by **Giulio Maestro**

Superdupers!

Really Funny Real Words

Too Hot to Hoot

Funny Palindrome Riddles

Guppies in Tuxedos

Funny Eponyms

I Think, I Thought

And Other Tricky Verbs

Mad as a Wet Hen!

And Other Funny Idioms

In a Pickle

And Other Funny Idioms

Your Foot's on My Feet!

And Other Tricky Nouns

Eight Ate

A Feast of Homonym Riddles

More Clarion Word Play Books by
Marvin Terban

Funny You Should Ask

How to Make Up Jokes and
Riddles with Wordplay

Hey, Hay!

A Wagonful of Funny
Homonym Riddles

Punching the Clock

Funny Action Idioms

The Dove Dove

Funny Homograph Riddles

About the Author and Illustrator

Marvin Terban has been teaching English for thirty years at Columbia Grammar and Preparatory School in New York City. His twelve previous Clarion Word Play Books began as language arts games in his classroom. Also an actor, Mr. Terban has appeared in community theater and films. In the summer he directs children's plays at a camp. Mr. Terban lives in Manhattan with his wife, Karen, their two children, and many pets.

Giulio Maestro attended the Cooper Union Art School, and has been illustrating and writing children's books since 1969. He and his wife Betsy have worked together on many books, including their most recent book for Clarion, *The Story of Money*. Mr. Maestro has collaborated with Marvin Terban on eight other Word Play Books for Clarion. He lives in Old Lyme, Connecticut.